ROLLERAMA

Jo Hinchliffe

Illustrated by Marina McAllan

sundance

For information regarding permission, write to:
Sundance Publishing
234 Taylor Street
Littleton, MA 01460

Published by
Sundance Publishing
234 Taylor Street
Littleton, MA 01460

Copyright © text Jo Hinchliffe
Copyright © illustrations Marina McAllan
Project commissioned and managed by
Lorraine Bambrough-Kelly, The Writer's Style
Cover and text design by Marta White

First published in 1996 by
Addison Wesley Longman Australia Pty Limited
95 Coventry Street
South Melbourne 3205 Australia
Exclusive United States Distribution: Sundance Publishing

ISBN 0-7608-4957-9

Printed in Canada

Contents

Contents

Chapter 1
A Crazy Household

My name is Cassidy Ferguson Bourne. I am going to be a famous skater one day. So is my dad, even though he is nearly fifty years old.

Fifty is very old for someone to be a champion. But Dad keeps telling us that he is a first-rate skater.

Dad used to ice skate on icy ponds in Norway and on ice rinks in Sweden.

He used to roller skate along the crowded streets of New York City.

He was a speed skater, too. He said he almost made the U.S. Olympic Team.

But never, ever, ever have we seen him skate.

Our family skates at the Rollerama every week. We beg Dad to come with us and show us his skills. But he always finds something he has to do.

It's hard to imagine Dad as a talented
person.

He seems to live in a world of his own. Some days even his socks don't match.

Because of Dad, we have two phone numbers. Dad always takes the cordless phone when he works in the garden. And usually he loses it. Then he has to dial the number of the cordless from the house phone.

Everyone runs outside to listen for the ringing that will lead us to the lost phone.

One day the hunt took two hours because the phone was ringing under a compost pile.

Dad is always losing things. Once he lost the car in a crowded parking lot. It took him all afternoon to find it. The ice cream melted all over the rest of the food in his shopping cart. What a mess that was!

Last week Dad was watching TV and said that the picture was way out of focus. It wasn't really.

He was wearing Grandma's glasses!

So it was very surprising to hear that Dad had a talent for skating. Especially a talent that we had never seen.

Last year, we were practicing hard for the Christmas show. But Dad said that he didn't need any practice. He said that he would do just fine with the talent he had already. He made a solemn promise that he would skate in the Christmas show. He promised to show us all the skills that had made him a champion.

Our mom is a little bit different, too. She wears the most amazing clothes. She thinks that getting dressed is a creative art.

One day she wore her latest garbage bag creation to our school.

That was the day she had lunch duty!

Another day she dressed up as a fruit bowl. She was going into the city and didn't want to bother bringing a lunch. By the end of the day, she had eaten most of her dress and smelled a lot like the vegetables in our refrigerator.

It will be truly amazing if I do become famous after growing up in such a crazy household.

Mom's favorite pastime is recycling. She can make something out of almost anything.

Our Christmas show costumes were proof of that.

For Dad's costume, Mom used a round lamp shade. She cleverly made it into a plum pudding. Dad didn't say much about his costume. Maybe he had wanted to be a present or a Christmas stocking.

We suggested pouring white sauce over Dad just before he made his entrance. But Mom made a fake sauce cover out of recycled lace instead.

My brother Nathan hated his costume. Mom said that because he was so thin, the only thing he could possibly be was a candle. She made a cardboard cylinder that covered him completely, except for his feet and ankles. She found an old flashlight for him to hold upward so the light shone through a tissue-paper flame.

He hated that his face was covered. So Mom gave in. She cut out eyeholes so he could see.

My sister Brigitte loved her Christmas bell costume. Mom made it out of colored crepe paper. Little bells hanging from a ribbon band would tinkle when Brigitte skated.

Since I am going to be a famous skater, Mom let me choose my own costume. I chose the fairy at the top of the Christmas tree. And guess who was the tree? Yep!

OUR MOTHER!

Mom pulled out all of last year's Christmas
tree decorations and sewed them onto a long
green dress. The dress fabric was our old
Christmas tablecloth. She spent days on this out-
fit. She even added colored lights to her tree
dress. Dad didn't seem at all impressed with
Mom's dress. He kept mumbling about having
to recharge her batteries during the show.

Chapter 2

Costumes, Costumes, Costumes

The night of the show finally arrived.

We spent nearly the whole day getting into our costumes.

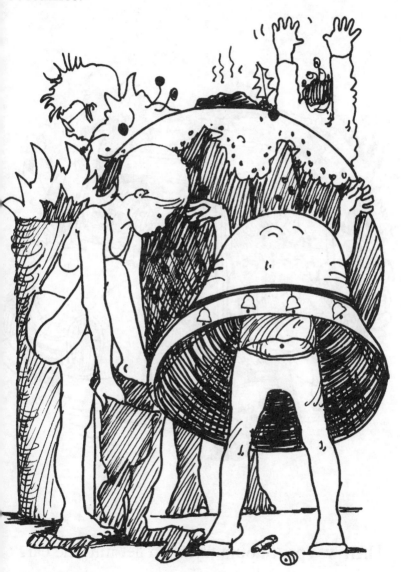

Then we spent hours trying to get into the car.

In the end, we put Dad on the roof rack. Plum pudding was just too big to fit in our car.

At last we all stumbled into Rollerama.

The rink was ablaze with flashing lights.
Excitement filled the room.

We made our way to a table near the rink.

Our plum pudding Dad made his way to the back of the snack bar. (I had told Mom days ago to cut eyeholes in the lamp shade so that Dad wouldn't get lost.)

Everyone in our skating club was there. Jason was wearing a stunning snowman costume. He had made it himself. A piece of carrot jutted out as a nose. Unfortunately, his dog had bitten the rest of it off just as Jason was going out the door.

People were dressed as bells and bonbons, stockings and sequin balls. Santas stuffed with pillows had huge sacks on their backs.

There was a parade of presents and partridges.
Tom and Sara were wearing red and green elf
outfits.

Before the show, there was an hour of skating games.

The Limbo Lower Game was first.

Nathan found it impossible to bend under the bar in his cylinder. Mom lost half of her tree decorations during her first bend.

Dad seemed to have disappeared. We couldn't see him anywhere.

The Magic Arrow game was next. But on the first spin, the arrow whizzed across the floor and went straight through Brigitte's paper hat. She looked like the apple on that boy's head in the William Tell story.

We missed Dad in the third game. He was
always good at Spinning the Bottle.

We were having a wonderful time!

Chapter 3

Our Hero, the Plum Pudding

Finally, the show began. The production was called *The Famous Flight of Santa Claus*.

Scene One took place at the North Pole. Mr. and Mrs. Claus were preparing for the flight ahead.

Tom and Sara skated right through a pile of presents. They landed on top of each other under the sleigh and eight reindeer.

Nathan managed to skate *The Dance of the Christmas Candle* without falling over, even though he could hardly move his feet under his cylinder.

Brigitte joined hands with five other bells. They skated to *A Tinkle of Christmas*.

The song they skated to kept repeating and they just kept on skating. You could hear their crepe paper costumes rubbing together. All of the bells were in tattered shreds when they finished.

It was nearly time for Mom and me to skate. We were doing *Oh Christmas Tree, Oh Christmas Tree.*

But where WAS Dad?

Our music started. Mom rolled onto the rink
with me sitting on her shoulders.

We were skating with ten other trees and fairies. Around and around we skated. I began to feel a little dizzy. Mom was getting hot in her costume and starting to lose her concentration.

Just as we came out of a very tight spin, I saw another tree and fairy coming straight at us.

What happened next seemed in slow motion.

From out of the corner of my eye, I saw a large plum pudding with Dad's head sticking out of the top. He was skating toward us.

A split second before we collided with the oncoming tree, we were on the plum pudding and being whisked out of danger. We had been saved from disaster by Dad!

Around and around the rink he skated with us on his plum pudding costume. It was hard to believe this was happening.

The crowd was clapping and stamping. Kids were cheering and waving streamers. Mom and I thought Dad would never stop.

When the three of us finally left the rink, Dad was the center of attention. He had pulled the lamp shade over his head again. So he missed the admiring looks everyone gave him. But I'm sure he felt all the pats on his pudding.

What a surprise for our family!

We drove home singing *For He's a Jolly Good Pudding.* Dad had to sit on the roof rack again because no one at the Rollerama could find scissors to cut him out of his costume.

When we arrived home, Mom found some scissors in the garage. We were finally able to give our hero the attention he deserved.

I am going to be a famous skater one day.
Just like my dad!

About the Author
Jo Hinchliffe

Jo has spent the last ten years developing her own language arts consultancy. She is a teacher, author, writer, artist-in-residence, poet, and mother. In between writing books for children and teachers, she now spends her time in schools working mainly as a poet. Jo has had 33 books published, including picture books, fiction and nonfiction books, teacher resource books, and blackline masters.